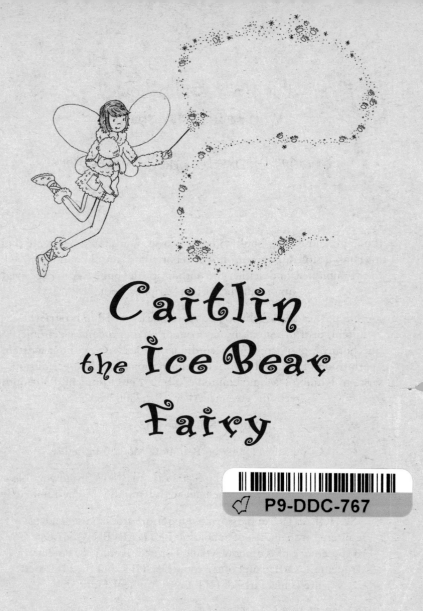

Caitlin
the Ice Bear
Fairy

For Holly Caitlin Powell,
who loves fairy stories

Special thanks to Sue Mongredien

ISBN 978-0-545-38424-7

12 11 10 9 8 7 6 5 4 3 2 1   12 13 14 15 16/0

Printed in the U.S.A.   40

This edition first printing, March 2012

Caitlin
the Ice Bear
Fairy

by Daisy Meadows

SCHOLASTIC INC.

New York   Toronto   London   Auckland
Sydney   Mexico City   New Delhi   Hong Kong

There are seven special animals,
Who live in Fairyland.
They use their magic powers
To help others where they can.

A dragon, black cat, phoenix,
A seahorse, and snow swan, too,
A unicorn and ice bear—
I know just what to do.

I'll lock them in my castle
And never let them out.
The world will turn more miserable,
Of that, I have no doubt!

Contents

Frosty Sparkles!

"I can't believe it's the last day of camp already," Kirsty Tate said sadly, as she finished packing her bag and zipped it shut. She gazed around the cozy wooden cabin where she and her best friend, Rachel Walker, had spent the week with four other girls. They'd been staying at an adventure camp and had taken part in all kinds of activities — exploring caves, canoeing, horseback riding — plus making some very special fairy friends!

The week of camp was almost over now, and their bunkmates had packed their bags and were ready to go home. Kirsty and Rachel were the only ones left in the cabin.

"We've had such amazing adventures this week," Rachel said, smiling as she thought about them.

Kirsty put on her jacket. "Well, our time here isn't over just yet," she reminded Rachel. "We're still going to climb High Hill . . . and we have to find the last magical animal, too."

Rachel nodded, an anxious expression appearing on her face. "Oh, I hope we find the little ice bear," she said. "I hate thinking about her being lost and alone."

"Or caught by Jack Frost's goblins," Kirsty added, frowning. "We can't let that happen."

It was kind of cold outside,

so Rachel grabbed their hats and scarves. "Come on," she said. "The sooner we get out there and start looking, the better!"

No one else at camp knew it, but

Kirsty and Rachel had been having some extra-special adventures . . . helping the Magical Animal Fairies find their missing animals! Jack Frost had stolen them, but the clever animals had found a way to escape from his Ice Castle and enter the human world, where they'd been lost ever since. So far, the two girls had helped the fairies track down a baby dragon, a magic black cat, a young phoenix, a seahorse, a snow swan, and a unicorn. But they still needed to find the ice bear cub.

Rachel and Kirsty went to meet the other campers, who were gathered outside the camp clubhouse. When everyone was there, one of the counselors, a tall man named Michael, spoke. "It's the camp tradition to climb High Hill together on the last day of the week," he said. "And when we get back, we'll have a special good-bye party. So if everyone's ready for the hike, let's go!"

A winding path led up the tall, grassy hill and the group set off together. They hadn't gone very far before they felt a cold wind begin to blow around them. "I'm glad I've got my gloves," Kirsty said, digging them out of her coat pockets. "It's chilly, isn't it?"

Rachel nodded, pulling her hat a little lower over her ears. "Yes—and look, there are even patches of frost on the ground up ahead," she said, pointing them out.

"Oh!" Kirsty said, walking faster toward them. Rachel had to jog a little to catch up with her, being careful not to slip. Kirsty seemed to speed up even more as they strode along the path.

Before long, the girls were a good way ahead of all the other campers.

Rachel glanced down and was surprised by how high they'd climbed. The camp already seemed small below them, and the staff preparing for the party looked like tiny stick figures.

Rachel almost slipped on a patch of frost and quickly turned her attention back to the path. "Maybe we should slow

down," she suggested, as Kirsty seemed to speed up even more. "It's very slippery here."

Kirsty shrugged. "We'll be fine," she said. "I feel like I could do anything!"

Rachel glanced at her friend in surprise. Kirsty was in a weird mood! But before Rachel could say anything, they heard Michael shout out behind them, "Girls, slow down! It's not a race! You guys are leaving the rest of us behind!"

Rachel turned to see Michael waving at them. "Find a spot to wait for the rest of the group," he called. "Let everyone catch up, OK?"

"OK," Rachel agreed, but Kirsty didn't seem to have heard.

"Rachel, look," she was saying urgently, grabbing her friend's arm. "Look at that shrub over there—it's covered in sparkles!"

Rachel glanced over to where Kirsty was pointing. Sure enough, the dark green bush was bright with tiny twinkling lights. Was it more frost or was it . . . ?

Before she could finish her question, a tiny fairy fluttered out of the shrub, with a trail of glittering fairy dust behind her. It was Caitlin the Ice Bear Fairy!

Too Late!

Caitlin had short brown hair and sparkly brown eyes. She was wearing a fluffy lilac coat with a furry pink collar, turquoise leggings, and big furry boots. "Hello, girls," she said. "I'm looking for Crystal, my ice bear. Have you seen her anywhere?"

"I'm sure we can find her," Kirsty said confidently. She put her hands on her hips. "Maybe I should climb a tree to get a good look around?"

Rachel gave her friend a confused look. "I'm not sure that's a good idea," she said slowly. "This part of the hill is so steep—if you fell, you could get really hurt."

"I won't fall!" Kirsty declared. Rachel stared at her. Kirsty was acting so strange today! "Are you all right?" she asked.

Caitlin smiled.
"I think I know
why Kirsty is
feeling so brave,"
she said. "It's
because of Crystal
the ice bear's magic—
she must be somewhere
nearby!"

Rachel smiled, too. Of course!
At the start of their adventure, she
and Kirsty had learned that each of
the seven magical animals had a
very special power—such as humor,
imagination, courage, and compassion.
The Magical Animal Fairies trained the
animals and taught them how to use
their powers, so the animals could spread
their gifts throughout the human world

and Fairyland. Crystal's power was the
gift of courage.

"Remember, a
magical animal's
power can become
stronger or
even work
in the opposite
way when they're
nervous or

scared," Caitlin reminded the girls.
"And their powers affect people
who are close to them!"

Kirsty looked excited. "So where is
Crystal?" she wondered aloud. "I can't
see her, but it's definitely cold enough for
an ice bear around here."

Just then, Caitlin let out a gasp and
pointed to a sparkling, icy trail that led

farther up the hill. "Look how thick that ice is," she said. "I have a horrible feeling that Jack Frost has been here. He must be searching for Crystal, too!"

Even Kirsty felt her confidence fade when she heard this. She and Rachel had

met cold, prickly Jack Frost many times
by now, and he was really scary. But
she hated the thought of little Crystal
being caught by him even more than she
dreaded seeing him herself. "We've got
to track them both down—and fast," she
said in a determined voice. "Maybe . . ."

"*Sssshh,*" Rachel
whispered, elbowing
her. The campers'
voices and laughter
were much
louder now, as
Michael and the
rest of the group
caught up with them.
Caitlin had to duck into
the folds of Rachel's scarf so that she
wouldn't be seen.

"We're going to take a short break,"
Michael announced to everyone. "It's
been a tough climb
and there's still a ways
to go before we'll
reach the top. I've
got a thermos of
hot chocolate here
and snacks, too.
Come and help
yourselves, then find
a quiet spot to take a break."

Kirsty raised an eyebrow at Rachel,
who nodded. This sounded like the
perfect opportunity to sneak up the
icy trail in search of Jack Frost! They
grabbed some cookies and set off at
once, carefully making their way up the
frozen path.

It was very slippery and both girls had to tread carefully, clinging to the shrubs on either side of the steep trail so they did not lose their footing. As she almost skidded for the third time, Rachel realized that Jack Frost might have made the path icy to keep them from finding Crystal. It wouldn't surprise her. He was so horrible!

Five minutes of slipping and sliding
later, the girls were so far up the path,
they could barely hear the sound of their
friends farther down the hill. The trail
twisted around the corner . . . and then
the girls stopped as they saw who was
standing only a few feet ahead: Jack
Frost! He had a little
white bear cub on an
icy leash and was
smiling in a
horrible, gloating
way.

"You're too late!"
he cried, his voice
ringing out through
the cold air. "The ice
bear is mine again.
Those silly goblins—I should have

known better than to trust them with
bringing back the magical animals. If
you want a job done right, you've got
to do it yourself. And now I have the
ice bear, and it will make me the most
courageous creature in Fairyland!"

Caitlin fluttered out from
her hiding place.
Her face dropped
with despair when
she saw Crystal
on a leash. The
ice bear growled
with unhappiness
when she saw her

fairy friend, and struggled to get free. But
Jack Frost simply pulled the leash tighter
so that Crystal couldn't move.

"You're making a mistake," Caitlin

cried, her voice shaking. "Stealing Crystal won't guarantee you courage—her magic doesn't work like that."

"Well, it's working just fine so far," Jack Frost snarled. "I feel full of courage—and confident that you'll never get her back again!" He waved his wand and was surrounded by glittering blue icy magic. In the blink of an eye, he and Crystal had completely vanished.

To Jack Frost's Castle

"We have to go after him," Rachel said, as the last blue sparkles from Jack Frost's magic faded. "Time will stand still here while we're in Fairyland, right? Let's try to find him there!"

"You're right," Caitlin agreed, her face pale. "We'll go to his Ice Castle right away!" She waved her wand and a flood of sparkly lilac fairy dust swirled around the three of them. It wrapped the girls in a glittering whirlwind and lifted them off their feet.

A few seconds later, they landed and
the whirlwind disappeared. Now they
were in Fairyland—and Kirsty and
Rachel had both been turned into fairies
with their own shimmering wings on
their backs!

Kirsty shook out her
wings with a smile,
then looked
around. They
were standing
in a snow-
covered garden
outside a tall
castle with icy
blue towers—
Jack Frost's
castle!

"My magic won't take us inside the

castle," Caitlin explained. "We'll have to sneak in somehow to see if Jack Frost is there." She fluttered her wings and rose from the ground. "Come on, let's fly around and see if we can find a way in."

The three friends flew high into the air and began circling the castle. Down below, goblins were running around and shouting. "There's a bear in the castle!" the fairies heard one cry with fear. "I saw it—and it had such sharp teeth! There's no way I'm going in there again!"

"That's interesting," Caitlin said, hovering in midair as she watched them. "It looks like Crystal's courage magic is working in reverse on these goblins. They seem awfully nervous." A hopeful expression appeared on her face. "I wonder if all this running around means they left the castle unguarded? We might be able to get in easily."

The three of them fluttered through the air, searching for a way into the castle. Unfortunately, the windows were all barred, and there were goblin guards on the towers. There were also two goblins at the huge doors that marked the main entrance to the castle. These goblins looked nervous about something, too, and the fairies flew closer so that they could listen to their conversation.

"Jack Frost is going to be really angry if he doesn't get his ice pops soon," one of them said fearfully. "But I refuse to go in the same room as that scary bear!"

"I heard it growling a minute ago," the second goblin said as he shook with fear. "What are we going to do?"

Rachel smiled as an idea suddenly came to her. "*We* could offer to take the ice pops in!" she hissed. "Caitlin, could you use your magic to make us look like goblins?"

Caitlin nodded. "Yes," she replied, her face lighting up. "Great idea — hopefully then we can get close to Jack Frost and Crystal, too. The only thing is, turning us all into goblin look-alikes will take a lot of magic, and the effects won't last for very long."

"Then we'll have to be as quick as we can," Kirsty said. "I think it's our only chance!"

Looking Green!

The three friends quickly found a
deserted corner of the castle grounds.
Caitlin waved her wand and muttered a
string of magical-sounding words. There
was a green flash of light and a swirl
of lilac fairy dust, and then Rachel and
Kirsty felt the strangest sensation in their
faces—as if their skin was stretching!

Kirsty reached up to pat her face and her eyes widened in surprise when she felt how long and bumpy her nose was. Oh, and her ears felt enormous!

She looked at the other two and burst into giggles. They were hardly recognizable as Rachel and Caitlin. They both looked just like sneaky green goblins!

"I don't know why you're laughing." Rachel giggled, elbowing her. "You're

not looking so pretty yourself!"

"We should hurry," Caitlin reminded them. "My magic won't last long, and Crystal's magic might be reversed any second. Then the goblins will be super-confident instead of nervous."

The three of them went quickly to the entrance of the castle, where the goblin guards were still arguing about the ice pops.

"We'll take them," Kirsty offered, trying to make her voice deep like a goblin's. Her heart pounded as she waited for them to reply. Would the disguise fool them?

The guards exchanged a sneaky look. "Sure," one said, pushing the box of ice pops over. "It's totally safe in there. There's no bear or anything . . . *ow!*" He yelped as the other goblin stomped on his toe.

Rachel pressed her lips together, trying not to smile. So far, so good! "Is Jack Frost in his throne room?" she asked.

"Yep," the second guard replied. "With that scary b—" He stopped quickly and covered his mouth. "With nothing," he said quickly. "He's in there with nothing."

"Fine," Kirsty said, taking the box. "Come on, guys."

Once past the guards, the three friends ran through the long icy corridors toward Jack Frost's throne room. They'd been inside the castle many times now and knew which way to go.

But as they hurried along, Kirsty noticed with a pang of fear that Rachel's hands were no longer as green as they had been. "I think the magic might be wearing off already," she said nervously. "Look at your hands, Rachel!"

Rachel peered down in dismay, then inspected Kirsty's face. "Your nose isn't as pointy as it was, either," she said. "We have to get there as soon as possible!"

"We need to work out our plan, too," Caitlin realized. "How are we actually going to get Crystal back, once we're in the throne room?"

"It's probably best if you free Crystal, since she knows you," Rachel said, thinking fast as they rushed along. "Maybe Kirsty and I can distract Jack Frost, so you have a chance to get close to Crystal?"

"I think that's a good idea," Kirsty agreed as they reached the throne room.

"Me, too," Caitlin said, taking a deep

breath. "Come on, then. Let's do it."

Kirsty knocked on the door and they walked in, trying to look as businesslike as possible.

Jack Frost was sitting on his icy throne, drumming his fingers on the armrest. Crystal was tied to the throne by an icy leash, and was lying with her head on her paws.

"Poor thing," Caitlin murmured under

her breath. "She looks so unhappy!"

The throne room was chilly and grand, lit by icy chandeliers and paved with a stone floor. Rachel could feel goosebumps prickling along her arms, and her teeth chattered in the cold. Jack Frost looked up at the new arrivals, and his eyes narrowed to slits. Rachel's heart skipped a beat. Did he recognize them?

Revealed!

Kirsty was worried at the sight of Jack Frost's expression, too. Then she realized he was staring at the box of ice pops. "About time!" he snarled. "What kept you?"

"Our apologies," Kirsty said, bowing respectfully.

"Well, hurry up and bring me a green pop already," he snapped, holding out his hand.

A thought struck Kirsty. Maybe this was a good opportunity to distract Jack Frost! She plucked a red ice pop from the box and took it to him, her heart pounding. "Here you go," she said.

Jack Frost glared at the red ice pop, then at Kirsty. "Green, you fool! I said green! This is red!"

Kirsty pretended to look surprised. "Red? It looks green to me, sir," she said in her goblin voice.

Rachel guessed what her friend was

44

up to. "I'd say that was green, too," she
agreed.

Jack Frost snorted.
"Are you both
color-blind? It is
red! And I want a
green pop. Goblin
green, like all of
you!"

Kirsty winced
a little when he
said "goblin
green." If
Jack Frost
looked closely at them, he would see
that they were looking less green by the
second. Caitlin's magic was wearing off
quickly now—too quickly for her liking!
Thankfully he seemed more concerned

with his ice pop than anything else at the moment, but she knew that could all change. . . .

"Is *this* green?" Rachel asked innocently,  holding up a yellow pop. Jack Frost groaned. "No, that's yellow," he replied. "Don't they teach you anything at goblin school? Get me a green pop—and get it now, before I really lose my temper!"

The argument went on like this for a few minutes, until Jack Frost finally snatched the box of ice pops out of Kirsty's hand. "I've had enough—I'll get one myself," he said, rummaging through them.

While his head was down, Caitlin
made a dash toward Crystal. She pulled
her magic wand out of her pocket and
pointed it at Crystal's icy
leash. It melted with
fairy magic
in an instant!
Jack Frost
was still so
busy sorting through the pops, he didn't
see a thing.

Caitlin smiled joyfully at the little ice
bear. "Hello, Crystal!" she said . . . but
the bear cub backed away from her
suspiciously.

"She thinks you're a goblin!" Kirsty
whispered to Caitlin. "You're going to
have to turn us back into fairies!"

She'd tried to say the words quietly,

but Jack Frost had excellent hearing. He snapped his head up at once, his eyes cold. "What did you just say?" he snarled, tossing the box of ice pops back at Kirsty. Then a furious expression spread over his face as he saw that Crystal had been set free—and that Caitlin had a fairy wand in her hand!

Kirsty and Rachel both felt frozen with fear. Thankfully, Caitlin moved like lightning, pointing her wand at the girls and then herself. Instantly, the three of them were all fairies again, able to fly up into the air and away from Jack Frost. He looked as if he might explode with rage!

"Come back here, you horrible fairies!" he yelled, reaching for his own wand.

Crystal, meanwhile, let out a happy-sounding rumble at the sight of her fairy friend and started to gallop toward her. She stopped short at the sound of Jack Frost's loud shout.

"I haven't finished with you yet," Jack Frost bellowed. He swished his wand through the air. Icy lightning bolts shot from its tip, crackling with magic as they hurtled toward Kirsty and Rachel.

"Look out!" screamed Rachel. "Duck!"

A Perfect Party

The lightning bolts were fast and
dangerous, and Kirsty and Rachel had
to dive and dodge to avoid being hit.
The ice bolts crashed against the walls
and smashed through the windows,
shattering the glass.

Kirsty was terrified as she swerved
back and forth. She knew that if she
was hit by one of the lightning bolts,
she wouldn't stand a chance!

But then Crystal let out a roar, showing all her sharp white teeth . . . and suddenly Jack Frost didn't look so confident anymore. In fact, when Crystal roared again and then growled, Jack Frost backed up against the wall and dropped his wand from his shaking fingers.

"He's terrified!" Rachel said to Kirsty. She'd never seen their old enemy look so frightened before. His lower lip was actually trembling, as if he were about to cry!

Caitlin winked at them. "Clever Crystal has used her magic—in reverse," she explained in a low voice. "Now Jack Frost has no courage at all. The magic won't last long, though, so we should get away while we can. Let's go!"

Crystal ran to her fairy friend, changing back to fairy-size as she went. Caitlin waved her magic wand, showering them all in a cascade of fairy dust. The glittery dust whipped up a whirlwind around them and whisked them away.

When they landed, they were outside the Fairyland Palace. As their feet touched the ground, Rachel and Kirsty saw that a crowd was there to greet them! There was Ashley the Dragon Fairy, Lara the Black Cat Fairy, Erin the Phoenix Fairy, Rihanna the Seahorse Fairy, Sophia the Snow Swan Fairy, and Leona the Unicorn Fairy—and they all had their magical animals with them. The king and queen of Fairyland were there, too. All the fairies cheered as they saw that Crystal had been safely reunited with Caitlin.

"You did it!" cried Ashley, and her baby dragon, Sizzle, sent a burst of flames into the air in excitement. "Nice work!" Lara smiled, her small black cat winding around her ankles and purring as loud as an engine.

"My dears," King Oberon said, smiling

and stepping forward. "Once again, you have helped us enormously. We are so grateful for all you've done, reuniting all our Magical Animal Fairies with their animals."

"And we're so proud of your bravery and quick thinking, too," Queen Titania added warmly. "Fairyland and the human world will both be better places now that our fairies can train the magical animals!"

"We'd like to throw a special party in your honor," the king said. "It's our way of saying thank you."

Rachel beamed at these words. "That sounds wonderful," she said. "But we should be thanking you!"

"Especially since we've seen how miserable life would be without the magical animals' gifts," Kirsty said. "It was horrible when I lost my imagination—I'm so glad the fairies are there to train the animals and spread their wonderful powers everywhere."

The Magical Animal Fairies all looked delighted by Kirsty's words. Then Kirsty and Rachel's old friends,

the Party Fairies, flew in to help
the king and queen work some
amazing party magic! Within
moments, the palace courtyard had
been decorated with huge bunches of
colorful balloons, twinkling Christmas
lights, and glittering streamers. A
Fairyland band played on a stage, with
Belle the snow swan singing a lively
melody.

Lucky the black cat was up on her hind legs, dancing with Twisty the unicorn. Giggles the phoenix swooped around telling jokes and making everyone laugh, while Sizzle sent bursts of fire into the air, creating wonderful fireworks. And, somehow, Bubbles the seahorse had arranged a spectacular water display in the fountain!

"This is amazing," Rachel said, gazing around in wonder. "It's the best party ever!"

Kirsty agreed. The walls echoed with the sound of laughter and singing, and everyone was smiling and happy. But once she and Rachel had danced with Lucky and Twisty, and eaten some of the delicious fairy party food, they knew they should get back to their own world.

"Thanks again for everything," Caitlin said, flying over and hugging them both. "You were amazing today— truly courageous,

even without Crystal's magic!"

"Thank you,"
Kirsty said,
stroking the
cub's soft white
fur. "I'm so happy
we could help you
rescue Crystal!"

"I've loved our
adventures with you
and the other Magical
Animal Fairies," Rachel
added, waving at their new
friends with a lump in her throat. "Bye!"

After the girls had said all their good-
byes, Queen Titania threw a handful
of glittering fairy dust over them. A
shimmering whirlwind picked them up
and took them back to the human world.

Kirsty and Rachel found themselves on High Hill again . . . and noticed almost immediately how much warmer it was there now. "That's because Jack Frost has gone," Kirsty said happily, looking around. "Isn't the view amazing from up here?"

Rachel agreed. There below them
lay the camp, surrounded by lush trees
and meadows. They could see the blue
lake, the winding river, and the rushing
waterfall, all sparkling in the sunshine.
"The world looks perfect," she said,
feeling very content.

Kirsty smiled. "The world *is* perfect, now that we've helped the Magical Animal Fairies find their animals!" she said.

Rachel slipped an arm through Kirsty's. "We'd better go and find Michael and the rest of the group," she said. "I guess we'll be going back for the camp party soon. Two parties in one day! We're so lucky."

"We are," Kirsty agreed. "We're the luckiest girls in the world." She smiled at Rachel, and then the two friends set off happily together. Another fairy adventure had come to an end!

RAINBOW magic™

THE PRINCESS FAIRIES

Another magical adventure is
just around the corner! Rachel and Kirsty
are about to meet the Princess Fairies, starting with

Hope
the Happiness Fairy!

Join their next adventure
in this special sneak peek. . . .

Princess Rachel and Princess Kirsty!

"We're here, Kirsty!" Rachel bounced up and down in her seat with excitement as she pointed out the bus window. "Look, that sign says GOLDEN PALACE."

Kirsty beamed at her friend. "I can't believe we get to spend a whole week in a *real* palace." She sighed happily. "I'm beginning to feel like a princess already!"

There were cheers and whoops as the other kids on the bus also spotted the sign. Golden Palace was in the country just outside of Wetherbury, where Kirsty lived. The house was open to the public, but Kirsty had never visited it before. During spring break the house was holding a special Kids' Week, and Kirsty had invited Rachel to come to Golden Palace with her.

"I can't wait to see our bedroom," Rachel said eagerly as the bus drove through the tall wrought-iron gates. "Imagine staying in a room that was once used by princes and princesses!"

"I wonder what activities we're going to be doing this week," Kirsty added. "I hope we get to try lots of princessy things!"

The bus drove over a drawbridge and then began to wind slowly through the enormous grounds. Like all the other kids on the bus, Rachel and Kirsty stared excitedly out of the window, straining to catch their first glimpse of Golden Palace. But there were lots of amazing things on the way to the house that caught their attention, too.

"Look, a petting zoo!" Kirsty exclaimed as they drove past a field of tiny Shetland ponies and little white goats. The girls could also see another field with horses and donkeys grazing, and pens of baby piglets, rabbits, and guinea pigs. "Aren't the Shetland ponies cute?"

"There's a lake over there," Rachel pointed out. The lake was surrounded by beautiful willow trees, and ducks and swans were gliding across the water. "And look at that greenhouse, Kirsty. I can see lots of orange and lemon trees growing inside it."

The bus passed a croquet field with hoops stuck into the grass, and then a very big, complicated maze made of tall green hedges.

"That maze has lots of twists and turns," Rachel whispered to Kirsty. "We might get lost in it and need some fairy magic to find our way out!"

RAINBOW magic™

SPECIAL EDITION

Three Books in Each One—
More Rainbow Magic Fun!

RAINBOW magic™

There's Magic in Every Series!

The Rainbow Fairies

The Weather Fairies

The Jewel Fairies

The Pet Fairies

The Fun Day Fairies

The Petal Fairies

The Dance Fairies

The Music Fairies

The Sports Fairies

The Party Fairies

The Ocean Fairies

The Night Fairies

The Magical Animal Fairies

Read them all!

■ SCHOLASTIC

www.scholastic.com

www.rainbowmagiconline.com

RMFAIRY5